The Giant and the Spring

English / Spanish

El Gigante y el Niño Primavera

The Giant and the Spring

El Gigante y el Niño Primavera

English/Spanish

Retold by Kuang-ts'ai Hao; Illustrated by Eva Wang
Spanish translation by Beatriz Zeller
Copyright © 1994 by Grimm Press
All rights reserved
This bilingual edition is co-published & distributed exclusively
by
Pan Asian Publications (USA) Inc.
29564 Union City Blvd., Union City, California 94587 USA
Tel: (510) 475-1185 Fax: (510) 475-1489

ISBN 1-57227-010-1

Printed in Hong Kong

The Giant and the Spring
El Gigante y el Niño Primavera

English / Spanish

Retold by Kuang-ts'ai Hao; Illustrated by Eva Wang
Spanish translation by Beatriz Zeller

Grimm Press

It was a cold, winter night. The air was frozen in a snowy storm.

In the midst of the storm, one could see the soft light from a lonely house on top of a hill. It shone like a lighthouse in the dark sea of snow.

In this house lived Uncle Giant. He read more than anyone else, and whenever there was a problem, the villagers came to him for help.

Era una noche fría de invierno. Una tormenta de nieve parecía haber congelado el aire.

A pesar de la tormenta, se divisaba la luz ténue de una casa solitaria en la cima de una colina. En ese oscuro mar blanco brillaba como un faro.

En esa casa vivía un gigante. Leía más que nadie y siempre que había algún problema, la gente del pueblo acudía a él para que les ayudara.

"Winter goes too slowly, and Spring comes too late..." Uncle
Giant sleepily sighed as he took out a book to read.

A cold wind crept through the crack of a window and Uncle
Giant shivered. Knock. Knock... Who was knocking on the
window? Uncle Giant looked out, and saw something like a
little bird perched upon a branch near the window.

"El invierno pasa muy lento y la primavera llega muy
tarde..." pensó el Gigante con un suspiro mientras sacaba un
libro para leer.

Un viento frío entró por la ventana y el Gigante tiritó.
Alguien golpeaba a la ventana... ¿Quién podía ser? El Gigante
miró hacia fuera y vió algo como un pajarito posado en una
rama frente a su ventana.

Uncle Giant walked closer to the window and rubbed his eyes. He could not believe what he saw! It was not a bird, but a little boy in a shabby cloak, trembling on the branch.

El Gigante se acercó a la ventana y se frotó los ojos. ¡No pudo creer lo que vió! Aquello no era un pájaro, sino un niñito con una capa andrajosa, tiritando sobre la rama del árbol.

Uncle Giant quickly opened the window and took the boy down from the tree, cradling him gently. The boy shook his head and cloak, and all of a sudden, new leaves appeared on all the plants in the house!

Uncle Giant gave the boy some hot food, then took him for a hot bath. Soaking in the warm water, the boy smiled. Suddenly, all the flowers bloomed!

Oh, spring had come to the house. The little boy was Spring!

El Gigante abrió rápidamente la ventana y bajó al niño del árbol meciéndolo suavemente en sus brazos. El niño sacudió la cabeza y de repente todas las plantas de la casa se cubrieron de hojas nuevas!

Luego de darle algo caliente de comer, el Gigante le preparó un baño caliente. En el agua tibia el niño sonrió y con eso florecieron todas las flores!

Había entrado la primavera en la casa. ¡Aquel niño era la primavera!

Uncle Giant tried to talk to Spring, but Spring only smiled. He pointed to the bookshelves, and Uncle Giant happily took a book down to read Spring a story.

When the story was finished, Spring fell asleep in Uncle Giant's arms. Looking at the sweet face, Uncle Giant felt so happy that he stayed awake the whole night.

El Gigante trató de hablarle al Niño Primavera, pero él sólo sonreía. El Gigante se dirigió hacia los estantes y sacó un libro para leerle un cuento al niño.

Cuando hubo terminado el cuento, el Niño Primavera se quedó dormido en los brazos del Gigante. Al contemplar ese rostro dulce, el Gigante se sintió tan feliz que no pudo dormir en toda la noche.

The next morning, the children in
the village saw Uncle Giant's house glowing
on top of the snowy hill. They ran up to see
what it was.

What did they see? They saw Spring's
bright light.

As the children stood amazed, they heard
an angry roar...

A la mañana siguiente, los niños del
pueblo vieron que la casa del Gigante
brillaba en la cima de la colina nevada.
Subieron corriendo para ver qué pasaba.

¿Qué vieron? Vieron la luz brillante del
Niño Primavera.

De pie ante tal asombro los niños oyeron
un rugido furioso...

"What are you doing here?" shouted Uncle Giant angrily.
"This is my house! Go away, you little brats!" Uncle Giant
waved his big arms, and all the children ran away in fright.

Bang! Bang! Uncle Giant shut all the windows tight.

Click. Click. He also locked up Spring's cloak in a box, and
put it high on top of his bookshelf.

"¿Qué hacéis aquí?" gritó furioso el Gigante. "¡Esta es mi
casa! ¡Váyanse mocosos!" El Gigante hacía grandes gestos con
los brazos y todos los niños huyeron asustados.

Con un estruendo el Gigante cerró todas las ventanas. Igual
ruido hizo cuando le echó llave a la caja en que metió la capa
del Niño Primavera que luego escondió encima del estante.

Spring knew Uncle Giant did not want him to leave, but he had to go. If not, how could the flowers bloom? The grass grow?

So, Spring had an idea. While Uncle Giant slept, he took out many books and stacked them up like a ladder. One, two, three... he would reach the box in which his cloak was kept.

Just then, Uncle Giant woke up. He took Spring down from the pile of books and hid the key to the box. Without his cloak, Spring could not leave. He was very sad.

El Niño Primavera sabía que el Gigante no quería que él se fuera, pero sabía que tenía que partir. Si nó, ¿cómo florecerían las flores? ¿Cómo brotaría el pasto?

Al niño se le ocurrió una idea. Mientras el Gigante dormía, sacó muchos libros y los apiló como si fuera una escalera. Uno, dos, tres y podría alcanzar la caja en que estaba guardada su capa.

En ese mismo instante, se despertó el Gigante. Bajó al Niño Primavera de la pila de libros y escondió la llave de la caja. Sin su capa el niño no podía partir. Estaba muy triste.

To cheer Spring up, Uncle Giant made a beautiful wooden horse for him. "All kids like toys. This horse will show Spring how much I love him," thought Uncle Giant.

But Spring did not even glance at the horse. He only stared silently out the frozen window.

Para alegrar al Niño Primavera, el Gigante le hizo un lindo caballito de madera. "A todos los niños les gustan los juguetes. Con este caballo le mostraré al Niño Primavera cuánto lo quiero," pensó el Gigante.

Pero el niño no se fijó en el caballo. Permanecía silente mirando por la ventana congelada.

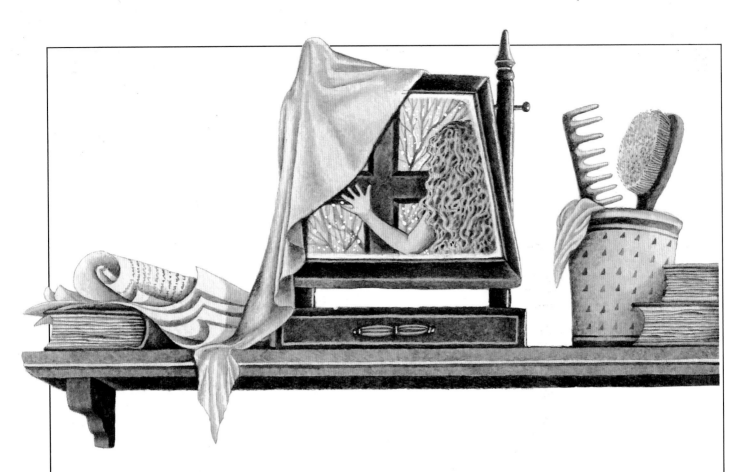

Spring spent all his time gazing unhappily out the window. Uncle Giant became unhappy, too. He said to Spring, "Do you hate me?" Spring shook his head slowly.

Uncle Giant said sadly, "I don't want to shut you in here, but if you leave me, I'll be lonely again. "

Spring said nothing, he only pointed out the window. Uncle Giant looked outside and saw the snow covered fields and houses. The villagers no longer came to visit anymore. The world was frozen and lifeless. The Giant's heavy heart sank ...

El Niño Primavera se pasaba las horas mirando con tristeza por la ventana. El Gigante también se entristeció. "¿Me odias?" le preguntó. El niño negó con la cabeza.

El Gigante dijo con tristeza, "no es que yo quiera mantenerte encerrado aquí, pero si tu te vas, volveré a sentirme solo."

El Niño Primavera no dijo nada. Sólo apuntó hacia la ventana. El Gigante vió el campo, vió las casas cubiertas de nieve. La gente del pueblo ya no lo venía a visitar. El mundo parecía congelado y sin vida. El Gigante sintió que se le rompía el alma...

The Giant turned around, and as he looked into Spring's sad face he heard a voice from deep inside him say, "You've kept Spring to yourself and left the world cold. You are tall, but your heart is small. Return Spring to the world, and fill your heart with love!"

Uncle Giant rushed to the bookshelf, took down the box, and carefully removed Spring's cloak. He patched up the holes in the cloak and put it on Spring.

El Gigante se dió media vuelta y al ver la cara de tristeza del niño, oyó una voz que venía desde muy adentro y que le decía: "Tú te has guardado al Niño Primavera para tí mismo y has hecho que el mundo permanezca frío. Eres alto, pero tienes el corazón pequeño. ¡Devuélve el Niño Primavera al mundo y tu corazón se colmará de amor!"

El Gigante bajó la caja que estaba encima del estante y cuidadosamente sacó la capa del Niño Primavera. Cuando hubo parchado todos los hoyos, se la puso al niño.

Uncle Giant opened the window. Spring smiled as if he was saying,
"Goodbye, my friend. I'll be back."
The snow stopped. The warm light of the rising sun shone on
Spring's cloak, and upon his face and eyes.

El Gigante abrió la ventana. El Niño Primavera sonrió como
diciendo: "Adiós amigo mío. Volveré."

Dejó de nevar. La luz tibia del sol de la mañana brilló sobre la capa
del Niño Primavera, sobre su rostro. Sus ojos se iluminaron.

Look! Spring is back in the world.

¡Miren! ¡La Primavera ha vuelto al mundo!

Since then, Spring comes back once a year to visit Uncle
Giant. And together, they enjoy a beautiful, warm season.

Desde entonces, el Niño Primavera vuelve una vez al año a
visitar al Gigante. Juntos los dos disfrutan de una bella y tibia
temporada.

About the Author and the Illustrator

Hao, Kuang-ts'ai (Author)

Hao Kuang-ts'ai is a rare talent in Chinese children's literature. In addition to editing, writing, and illustrating, he is also skilled in layout and design. With his talented artistry, strong intellect and childlike playfulness, he has produced a series of superb books.

Hao understands children. His stories are fluid and relaxing when read aloud and can be easily recited by children who enjoy the aesthetics of language and sound.

Hao Kuang-ts'ai was born in 1961 in Taipei, Taiwan. He graduated from the Law School at National Chengchi University before becoming an author of children's books. His book Wake Up, Emperor! won a top prize for children's literature and his other works also enjoy high acclaim.

Wang, Eva (Illustrator)

Eva Wang is a prominent figure among China's new generation of children's illustrators. She was born in Penghu, Taiwan in 1964.

Miss Wang's special talent first enjoyed international recognition in 1991. Her work, The Lazy Man Becomes a Monkey, won the first prize in the "First Biannual Asian Exhibition of Children's Book Illustrations", and her work in Seven Magic Brothers was shown at the "International Exhibition of Children's Book Illustrations in Bologna." Experts on children's literature worldwide highly praised this new illustrator from the Far East.

Before she began to earn her international reputation, Miss Wang had built a name for herself in Taiwan. She has become known for the richness and precision of her drawing and for her tireless attention to detail. She is one of those rare illustrators whose works can be appreciated from many perspectives.

Miss Wang's work demonstrates startling imagination and an abundance of child-like delight. Her drawings take children on a journey to a world full of love and beauty, a world from which they are reluctant to leave.